Moving

7 stories of women moving
from fear and despair to hope and courage

By Maida Berenblatt, M.S.

Forward

Everyone has a story. Along my journey, I have heard many stories from courageous and resilient women who were determined to find a way to be valuable, worthwhile and lovable, especially to themselves.

Walk with me, hear their struggles and rejoice in the their courageous achievement to be "somebody."

Hear Paula's cries to feel the pain of family loss to Marcie's search to find her lost daughter in the throes of addiction. See Zoe discover that she is a valuable, worthwhile and lovable woman. Struggle with Mirabelle's search for her father only to find her own true love, at last. Scream with Jenna as she fights to overcome the disease of alcoholism and find sobriety. Listen to Lauren's story of keeping the distance between patient and doctor. Feel the frustration of a personality disorder seeking to complete herself with many different personas. And at last, release the joy as you join each woman in her discovery of the rhapsody of an authentic self,

Mirabelle

The beginning of my story crosses two nations, Vietnam and America.

My mother Lang (which means orchid in our language) was an assistant to the cook of the American Ambassador outside the city of Saigon. Ever since I can remember, I was the assistant to the assistant. I never knew my father.

I heard, "Get this." "Hold that." "Put this down." "Lift this up." "Wash." "Dry." "Find." ... I certainly learned to be a very good assistant. Soon, I was able to stand on a chair over the sink, and wash vegetables and fruit, mix things in a bowl, and even pick flowers from the garden. By the time I was 10 years old, I learned to peel, chop, slice, and place food on the plates.

Finally, I got the courage to ask Mom one of my secret questions when she seemed to have a happy face.

"Tell me, where is my father?"

"Away."

"Please tell me who my father is?"

"No one you know."

"Please tell me if I will ever see him?"

"No."

"When you knew him, did you love him?"

"Go get the broom and sweep, now!"

That was the end of her happy face. After I did that job, I went into the corner to slurp poh, my favorite noodle soup.

As I got older, I came to this understanding by myself. I was born about one year at the end of the Vietnam War on May 1, 1976. I think my father was an American soldier who met my mother. The reason I think this is so, because I cannot find anyone in my village, Binh Chanh, with blond curly hair, just like me. Absolutely no one.

One day, the Ambassador had some very important guests from America. My mother and I made the best dinner by ourselves because the cook was sick.

The dinner was turtle soup, ginger sautéed frogs legs, roast chicken with rice and bean curd, and the best wine. For dessert we made broiled banana, marinated plums and pears with vanilla custard. Everyone said that it was the best dinner.

I don't know what happened that night, but the next morning Mother told me we were going to America.

At first, I cried a lot because I was scared. My whole world was to be turned upside down. When the day finally came, it was raining hard and a grey sky was all around us as we rode to the Noi Bai Airport, and I cried again. I had never been on an airplane before.

Then the idea came to me that maybe I would find a man with blond curly hair like me, and he would be my father.

The plane ride was very long, but I got to have my mother by my side the whole time; she never left me. When we got to a place called Logan Airport, we had another long ride to Brookline. Doctor and Mrs. Longwood's house was even bigger than the ambassador's house. It was like a castle from my childhood stories. The room that was given to us was the biggest I had ever slept in. We even got separate beds.

There I was in the kitchen again with my mother. Only this time, I had to learn the names of everything in English, but this language was so different. In the Vietnamese language, everything has one tense, only the voice makes the meanings change. Learning the past and future tenses in English was confusing and mix-ups were easy.

One night there were three special guests for dinner: Dr. Caliente, Mr. Rowe and a beautiful young lady, named Ariana, their daughter.

They loved our banh chung, sticky steamed rice stuffed with pork and egg wrapped in banana leaf.

Time passed and everyone said that I had grown into a lovely girl. I went to school to prepare for my citizenship test. On my 18th birthday, I heard that Ariana had married, and she needed someone in her home to take care of her soon to be born baby. I learned that I was to have my own family and my own job. Once again, I was scared, but Mother promised to call me and see me every week. She never missed our date.

Before I left the house, she told me the story of my father.

My mother was riding her bike to the market. It was very crowded and there were many people in her path. She tried to wiggle out of the way of the soldiers, but bumped into one man and fell to the ground. One of the spokes tore her white ao da (her pantsuit) and her conical hat fell off. The young man immediately helped her to her feet and said that he was so sorry, so many times. He insisted they stop for tea, so she could recover and rest. His name was Mick Bell, a blond curly haired Irishman from South Boston. "We had a good feeling with each other and met many times together before he was to be stationed up North. We spoke of marriage, and he said that he would come back for me to go home to the USA together, as soon as the war ended."

"After a few months, the letters stopped coming and then nothing, no word- 'Bell Missing in Action,' the US reported. Maybe he was not missing and maybe he went home without me. I still do not know. I am here in Boston to look for him."

That was my mother's story.

Well, I passed the test to be a US citizen and went to classes to improve my English.

When JR was born, we spent wonderful years together, and we both learned to speak and read English together. The family was wonderful to me and I felt as if I really belonged to them.

By the time JR was in junior high school, I went to Ariana and told her I had passed my GED.

More good news, I told her.

I met a man in my class with blond curly hair from Ireland and we wanted to belong to each other. My mother says that he is fine for me.

Since JR was in junior high school, he didn't need me anymore. It was another difficult separation but for a happy reason. I was to be married.

Ariana told me that I was a gift to her family, and wished me all the happiness in the world.

We did not visit or speak for many years. I had my job as an ESL teacher and was very busy with two sons and a wonderful husband.

One night, very late, I got an unexpected call from Ariana, telling me that JR was in Mass General Hospital with his girlfriend, Paula, who almost died and was still in a coma. He was wild with pain and could I come as soon as possible. She was sorry to call, but said that I was the only one who could offer him any comfort. One hour later, I placed my hand on his shoulder and he sobbed in my arms. I whispered his favorite lullaby, "*Demain Sera Meilleur.*" Yes, he did remember the many nights I sang that song to him, tomorrow will be better.

As the night passed, we talked about the years passed since we were together. I told him how wonderful my husband was, and a great father to our two sons. We now live in the suburbs where he manages a repair shop for sports cars and I am an ESL instructor at our local library. I feel blessed with this life. So many times I wanted to call and speak with you, but since you were grown up, I didn't think you needed a nanny.

JR, you know that I know about loss. I have lost my father and no longer look for him. He went away, but I still believe his love remains. My heart was open and I found love with my husband. I remember reading a poem by a Peruvian poet, Cesar Vallejo that has stayed with me. I do not remember the exact words, but the meaning is clear: when someone passes through your life, that person remains because that place is no longer empty.

I believe you and Paula will be together again. Keep your heart open and your love for her remains. I know you to be all goodness, but pout when you cannot have your way. Please call me as soon as you have some news.

Mirabelle gave him a loving hug and slipped her phone number in his jacket pocket.

Just Another Story

As Marcia walks along a perfectly manicured lawn with a border of multi-colored poppies, she notices the freshly painted, red shutters on the white house.

She clicks the brass knob and opens a thick, wooden door. Nestled in an upscale neighborhood, you would never know this is a residential treatment center for addicts. And, you never admit you have the disease of addiction, until you cross the threshold.

It is Sunday, family visiting day for clients in recovery. As a seasoned counselor, Marcia's job is to meet with families to explore the ways in which they can be most helpful in the process of a client's recovery. It is never easy. Sometimes she has a private session with a client in crisis or with the family who is resistant to change.

It is 9 o'clock, time to check on any new admissions.

Joe came in with a status of homeless; he used to work for a major firm on Wall Street. Abby has just lost her child to Child Protective Services (CPS), and she can't even remember where she last left her. When Chuck finishes his court mandated stay, the judge will determine just how many years he will be incarcerated; he is 18 years old. It was painful to look at Jane, and note how the cirrhosis of her liver has progressed; her eyes are yellow. Katie has just lost her catering business. She never thought about the drug world until she experienced heroin and spent two years chasing her first high.

It's onto the nurse's station to check the new admission. "You'd better see this one; she's in bad shape, still detoxing. We're not sure about the reliability of her history since no psychosocial was taken last night."

Marcia wonders if she should see this client or perhaps pass her on, but she soon discovers all the other counselors are busy.

I am not up to meeting this client as she walks to the conference room where a nurse is waiting with this woman. Marcia is a fifty-year-old divorced woman who is simply tired. I'll just take the history and move on. She is thinking to herself, no time for any drama; after all, it is just another story.

As soon as Marcia opens the door, her jaw drops; no sound or breath emerges from her mouth. She freezes. She faces a very fragile woman with tangled, disheveled hair and red, swollen eyes. This is no ordinary client.

Marcia is facing the daughter who she has not seen in ten years.

This one is not just another story.

The two women stare at each other for a moment- which seemed so much longer- until Marcia broke the silence, whispering, "Paula."

"Mommy," her eyes fill, and tears trickle down her pale cheeks, as Paula sobs.

Marcia reaches out and cradles her daughter in her arms and cries, "I am so happy to see you. I didn't even know you were alive."

Paula was so emaciated that Marcia's arms cradled shoulder blades and a rib cage.

"Neither did I. I don't want to die; I want to live."

Her cries become softer; her breathing eases as she sits down to face her mother's questions.

"What happened? You didn't call after you left."

Paula begins to tell her mother the story.

"We went to live with his friends in their trailer. We were pretty high most of the time. Then I got sick, and we made a pact to get clean. We went to meetings, got a sponsor, and he even got a job so we could move out. It was tough. I didn't feel strong enough to call. He relapsed. I slipped too, and we were both in trouble again. I wanted to leave, but I wasn't sure if I loved him or the drug he gave me. Then things got out of control. He overdosed and died. I don't want to die."

Marcia looks at her daughter--the sores on her arms, nails bitten down to the skin, a devastated, shrunken body~ and her heart aches.

"Paula, the breakfast program ends in fifteen minutes. It will be good for you eat something. I'll get another counselor to take your history and make a call for someone to take you to the dining room."

Marcia knows she needs to stop shaking before leaving this room. So many thoughts and feelings scramble for attention as she realizes that a boundary has been crossed from a professional concern for a client to a personal investment.

Alone in the room, Marcia collects her thoughts and recalls the memories of the past ten years. We were not good parents to Paula, and the divorce was ugly and spiteful. We were never friendly during those bitter years, why should I have expected him to befriend me? He never contributed enough money for child support. I had to work two jobs just to make ends meet. The arguments with Paula about her boyfriend were senseless and ended in tears and confusion. Finally, she left and went to live with him. I was powerless to change things.

I was unaware of the intensity of her drug use or even where she was living; she never called. I called her friends; no one gave me any information.

How many emergencies can one woman cope with?

Marcia had to dry her eyes and blow her nose. Enough! Did I not spend many therapeutic hours to resolve my guilt? One thing I know for sure is that I neither have the power to cause, control, or cure addiction. Will there always be nagging doubts? Can I ever be free of my fears that I am part of her problems? It is heartbreaking to see that Paula is now just a ghost of herself.

Stop! If I continue to focus on the past, I'll never be able to deal with the present.

I have to go to the bathroom and pull myself together and go back to work. My one strong coping skill- going to work!

One question remains unanswered; someone has to leave this center to experience a successful recovery for both mother and daughter? Who is the patient?

Paula's history is taken by Ben, assistant to the director. Nothing extraordinary is revealed with the exception that she is the first-born daughter of a staff counselor.

Paula's affect is rather flat as she reports her position in the family and her relationship with two younger siblings whom she often felt responsible for when her mother was not at home. Her sister Cassie, a cancer survivor, received all of the attention.

"I never even had a cold, she whispered. The divorce was tough; I stayed in my room and wrote a lot of poetry. It all seems silly now, but the collection's title reveals my feelings: "Holding onto a breaking branch." I was in a lot of pain, and I discovered quite by accident that a little stuff could quiet the pain. Then I met people who had a lot of stuff."

"All of a sudden, I wasn't so lonely, and I left home to party without restrictions. I was very young, and now I see, very foolish. One night, I just left."

Paula continues to report her experimentation with different drugs and how she lived in a group house with selling, using, abusing connected to needing, finding and using, until the cycle starts all over again.

"My turning point came when I got sick, and I held the hand of my boyfriend as he died. I want my life back. I want to live."

Paula listens as the program guidelines are read to her. Papers are signed, and she is assigned to a bed, a counselor, and a group. When she completes her detox treatment, she'll transfer to another facility.

Late that afternoon, Marcia is called to meet with the program director and his assistant, Ben.

Marcia is prepared, but a twisted knot in her stomach says she is scared. She remembers being this scared when Paula left home.

"We have an opening in our extension out east for Paula. As a parent, you'll be welcome to visit on Family Day but not privy to the counselor's records."

At this point, Paula's blood test for HIV infection has not come back from the lab.

Marcia nods and says that she understands. Her eyes fill, but she does not cry. She says, "I am hopeful for a recovery for both of us. Thank you."

The Empty Loft

"How could we let you go? Why didn't you hold onto us? You were everything to us, life itself. And in the end, as always, death took it all away." Twenty-three year old Paula is standing in front of her house in Sagaponack and talking to the 'For Sale' sign perched on the front lawn. She walks to the front door, struggles with the key in the lock, and walks inside with her constant companion, sadness.

"Standing in this empty room in an empty house that once held everyone I have ever loved, and everything I have ever known. It all demands more courage and strength than I have today. I had to come back, just once more before it's too late."

Once again, she is talking aloud to herself as she starts to weep. "It feels as if my arms are missing, no hugging and no one to love. The pain is unbearable. I can't stop crying."

Her footsteps echo on the hardwood floor as she walks through the empty dining room and living room, but they become quiet as she enters the beige carpeted sitting room. Sitting down on the paisley colored, velour bench around a large curved bay window, she gazes outside at the garden, which is sprinkled with a light layer of freshly covered snow, a December regular. Paula remembers one wintry morning when she found her mother, Jackie sitting by that same bay window with a coffee mug in hand, as she often did. She looked at Paula and sighed, "It's so remarkable how the early morning light actually changes the shape of our garden as the shadows play with different forms of..." Her thoughts were not finished as her dad Roy came in and talked about their dinner guests for that evening. They entertained a lot. "Just business," Roy always said. When he left, Paula curled up next to her mom and asked, "What was it really like to be an artist in New York City and live in that wonderful world of color and form? Did you work in a gallery?

How about all those art shows in the studios and the museums? I want to know all about that life."

"Honey, I put all that aside when I met Roy. Our marriage and raising you two girls were our top priority. Of course, Roy was not the type of man who would block anyone's dream. I changed the script and closed the door on any classes or studies when we moved to Long Island. That door was shut, bolted. Supporting Roy and his career became my goal. When you girls were born, I was simply too busy."

Leaning back against the wall, Paula pulls one of the cushions to her chest and begins to sob again; "I have to find something of her world in the loft: supplies, sketches, a palette, anything that she left behind and could be a connection to my anchor. Mom, I promise to keep it going. I'll keep the door open and continue painting."

Wiping the tears away with her sweater edge, she remembers another cherished memory, her last dinner with the entire family. It was five years ago when she turned a magical eighteen on May 11th, the summer before leaving for Boston University to pursue a major in Fine Arts. Jackie had just made Paula's favorite: a succulent roasted Long Island Duckling with beach plum sauce, braised Brussels sprouts and mounds of garlic, mashed potatoes, and the sweetest garden tomatoes a top freshly picked romaine lettuce, cucumbers all dressed in a rich macadamia oil, with balsamic vinegar seasoned to perfection. After dinner, her sister Mara, four years older than Paula, had just brought the birthday cake to the table. All eyes competed for a glimpse of the message on the vanilla cream topping. It was a tradition in the Blake family to find a funny and unique message for each celebration. While everyone expected a cake, the message was the big surprise. That night, it was Mara's turn to create the big surprise: "Bon Voyage Olaf!" Peals of laughter made it tricky for Paula to blow out the nineteen candles. Paula asked, "What happened to Mara? Olaf cancelled his trip and the cake was on sale?" The funniest message could inspire a comic response and then, more laughter.

Paula rocks back and forth, hugging the cushion as many more memories flash before her. This memory unfolded to another one in August of that same year, before Paula was to leave for Boston. All familiar faces, except one, her dad Roy had died that summer of congestive heart failure at the age of seventy-one. He never told anyone there was a problem. The family knew that he was under treatment for diabetes, but not heart disease. No one was prepared for this sudden loss. At the reading of Roy's will, his lawyer read a letter to his family. "My devoted, loving wife and two wonderful daughters were my life. I stayed as long as possible. Please live that life that belongs to you. I am deeply grateful for your unconditional love and the privileged life I have had."

Two weeks later, Paula left for school in Boston without a trace of excitement or anticipation of what was to come.

"I am all cried out; where is everyone?" She stares out the window and remembers that in her sophomore year at school, the family dinners ended. Jackie had died of an accidental overdose of sleeping pills. This memory leaves her numb. When Paula returned home for the funeral, she was ready to quit school and just stay in Sagaponack. All she could do was cry, sleep fitfully, and cry again. Mara assumed all the responsibilities for family and friends. Mara insisted that she return to school and keep her dream alive as her parents would have would wanted. In time, and with bereavement counseling, Paula was able to return to school, graduate, find an apartment and a job in an art gallery on Newbury Street.

"I have to get up," she moans, "have to get to the loft. Something has to be there." She moves slowly, as if disabled. Every muscle in her body painfully stretches to the next push and pull as she climbs the stairs from the first to second floor, and the across the hallway to another set of steps leading to the loft. The door does not open easily, and she uses all of her strength to push open the door. The smell of musty dampness forces her to sit down on the first box. Jackie was very organized and each box was labeled. This all has to be cleaned out before the closing next week. Sitting on a small trunk, her crying softened to a whimper, as she looked at the marked boxes: summer, winter, fall, spring, holidays, Roy, Jackie, Mara...all passes away. No need to examine the contents of these boxes, she neither wants or needs anything in the marked ones. She is desperately looking for something unmarked. She begins to move things around, whispering, "what will it look like?"

Paula walks to the window, glances outside the loft and notices that the snowflakes have stopped falling. A white blanket covers

Jackie's garden. Turning around, she sees one small file cabinet in the far corner of the room, unmarked. She holds her breath and thinks, "This could be it." The clasp was too tight to open. She runs down the stairs to the basement, hoping to find some tools. Finding nothing, she runs upstairs and out to the trunk of her car. Roy always insisted that she carry a small tool box, just in case. She races up to the loft again and begins to jiggle the clasp to pry it open. Finally, it opens; she moans, "Oh no, just another collection of cookbooks and national geographic magazines." Frantically, she tears through the papers only to discover a large canvas bag molded to the bottom of the file box. Her heart was beating fast and her hands shook. "Steady, steady," she whispers, "This could be it." She feels the sensation of being unable to breathe. "I have to get this bag downstairs. This is it. Yes, this is it."

While the canvas bag was not heavy, Paula was shaking and needed to hold one hand on the wall for balance. Finally, sitting on the living room floor, prying open the canvas bag which seemed to have been closed since 1972, was not easy. She slowly prodded the clasp open, success.

Here was the treasure: boxes of watercolors, tubes of acrylics, paint thinner, cloths, sponges, and brushes in all sizes and shapes. There were three rolls of lightweight canvas paper, all tied together with a purple string. The edges of the sheets had turned yellow from age, but there was a painting of Central Park in Manhattan. It was still quite vivid along with the skyline of the buildings at dusk. On the bottom of the bag was a letter that appeared to have been unopened. The date on top of the letter was the year and the month that Jackie became Mrs. Roy Blake. Opening the letter, Paula discovered that Jackie had been accepted to the New York School of Art and Design. Paula remembers her mother's words, "That was then; this is now. That door is bolted."

The sun is fading. Shadows fall across the floor and the setting sun changes from gold to butter to pink apricot as it slips behind the horizon. She feels a chill throughout her whole body. After placing each item back in the bag, Paula gets up to return to her apartment in Boston. She starts the car for a welcome burst of heat and looks longingly at the house of yesterday's memories.

On the drive back to Boston, Paula recalls another night of her birthday celebration when her sister Mara was late to the dinner. Mara burst through the kitchen door and squealed, "Sorry I'm late; our team won, so much to celebrate. I did remember to pick up the cake at the bake shop." Jackie retorted, "Mara, you are covered with dust from head to toe with straw sticking out of your pony tail. Take a quick shower and help with the dishes. I really appreciated the stop for the cake. It is a wonder that you remembered."

Mara had well defined features with a 5'8" body, trim and fit. Her warm brown eyes were framed with soft auburn curls, often pulled back in a ponytail. Mara knew that Paula was the family beauty and that was indisputable. She cherished her big sister role. Of course, all the excitement was at the Bridgehampton Polo Club event of the summer season. It represented the height of fashion, attracting the wealthy and powerful international jet set. Even the royals attended. One hundred and ninety ponies are flown in from Argentina and Europe along with their riders and fans. Mara's team was assigned to one of the riders and his horses. Their job was to keep the ponies refreshed and shaded between the chuckers, when the riders took a break and changed horses. Not only was this fast paced game exhilarating to watch, but winning went beyond expectations. Mara was floating on a cloud.

Paula stops in Connecticut for a refill and restroom. Once again, she breaks into a gasping sob, remembering the day that Mara was hit by a car while riding her bike. Pieces of her life remained fragmented when Mara was gone. After the phone call, Mara's death left her numb with grief; her world was empty. Days, weeks, and months passed, and she spoke to no one but herself.

How can she erase the family pictures in her mind? How can she move on and close this chapter of the deep sadness she is feeling"

By the time Paula reaches the Massachusetts Turnpike, she is imagining various frames for her mother's painting, something muted with a soft grey frame. Whispering to herself, she says, "I'll keep the door open and continue painting."

Her cell phone rings and jangles her frayed nerves. She knows the number and the questions from Jonathan: "How are you doing? When are you coming back? Hurry, I miss you so."

Her Name Is Everyname

Four women are having an end of summer gathering to share what has happened lately and what they are planning for the coming season. Lara Davidson, an adjunct professor in business at a local community college is hosting the party on her patio. Her guests include

Rita McCloud, an independent real estate broker in NYC who summers on the east end of Long Island.

Claire Denning, a CEO and founder of a business called "Start UP", lives full time of the East End.

Marcie Blake, a successful travel agent, summers on the East End and coordinates two offices in NYC and the Hamptons.

While they were all good friends; their professional and personal lives left little time for casual gatherings. The end of summer and of September was agreed by all four friends to stop what they were doing and reconnect, again. The caterers had left a sumptuous buffet of appetizers and munchies before dinner on the patio while Laura filled glasses with red and white wines, along with a champagne toast to the golden colors of fall. The women personified optimal wellness planning for good health. They were slightly tan, slightly botoxed, moderately tight and toned. They looked as good as any celebrity who visited the East End. They wore the money they earned, polished their hair colors along with coordinating colors on their toes and fingertips. They were successful women of the 21st century.

Marcie started with litany of woes, two busy offices along with an online website. "Be careful what you wish for," she moaned. I have hired extra staff but I need a clone. Someone who can deal direct with the traveler and sell the best offering. Then, out of the blue, a gorgeous blonde walks in and asks if she can intern in my office. We chatted, ate lunch together and she was taken in as part of my team. "Let me earn my salary, prove myself and then we can talk money," she said. It was almost too good to be true. She was consistently reliable every single day for one month. She handled the online business and international tours. Our office won a trip to South Africa for three weeks all expenses paid in the finest hotels. I felt that I should compensate in some way and gave her the trip to show my appreciation. At first she declined the offering, but when I persisted, she accepted. The night before she was to leave, I took her to dinner and gave her expense money with my complements for a job well done. She was a wonderful gal and to my amazement I liked her very much, as if I had known her for years. She gained my attention and my trust. Sometimes I wondered if I was actually attracted to her—the way she moved her head and her body when she walked about the office. Her clothing always accented her body- full bosom, waist curved around sensuous and swaying hips. I just laughed at myself for I have always desired a man, not a woman. She kept in touch during her travels with texts and photos. I found myself fantasizing about her return and reconnecting again. Finally her return date was here. OMG, what was I thinking? Was I even thinking? When I was caressing my body, her face was in front of me. I was hoping she would call right away, but I heard nothing from her. Maybe jet lag had set in. I began to call her, frantically, every hour on the hour. Finally, the telephone message stated that this number was no longer in service. I ran to her apartment only to discover that she no longer occupied this address. I sat in my car and cried asking myself repeatedly, "What happened? Where did I slip? Who is this woman that I trusted?"

Claire responded. "Oh, what a terrible experience for you. What was her name?"

"Sally Mimosa"

The gals were quiet while Lara served appetizers and refilled their drinks.

"Y'know, a cloud passes over our space to clear the way for sunshine," Rita continued. "I have always been optimistic and felt better on the sunny side, until a recent experience clouded my space. At a conference for women in business, I heard a presenter talk about moods and money. I felt this presented was directly related to me. I am guilty of using money, aka shopping to give me a lift. But when the unexpected expenses arise, I am short. I listened very attentively and said to the gal sitting on my right, "I've got to make a change now. My son is going to college next fall; I have to make his tuition." She smiled and said, "Maybe visualizing him on campus will give you enough of a lift to bank the money." "Wonderful idea," I responded. We didn't speak for a while and continued listening. Then I turned to her and said, "I earn a living as an independent real estate broker and I always think the river money will flow to me. It has always been that way; but now I am concerned."

"Do you have an accountant?" "Of course, for my business but not specifically for me."

"Let's talk during the break; I have an idea." She was very warm and engaging in a high-end designer suit, carrying a Birkin bag and wearing the latest Manolo shoes. It wasn't just the pink gold and diamond watch that caught my eye, but the large emerald ring with matching emerald drop earrings that were outstanding. I looked down at my simple skirt and sweater and felt dowdy. I really didn't have time to dress this morning and even if I did; it wouldn't be like that. She had me laughing at a joke about money and madness. Then she spoke of her fund in tax haven trading. Sounded very interesting I thought and would need more information over our cocktail hour.

"What happened next?" asked Lara as she brought a big salad bowl and plates to the table.

"By the end of our conversation, I was in. Why it wasn't even illegal. At the end of the meeting, I went home feeling very lucky, indeed. She gave me her card and we agreed on a weekly sum from my commissions with a summary report every two weeks. I was thrilled. Maybe I wouldn't have to take a second mortgage on my summer place, after all. As promised, the reports were steady, every two weeks. We didn't meet again, just emailed and texted. The reports came in steadily just as my money went out steadily."

The vision of seeing my son in college instead of another sweater in drawer worked quite well. I was feeling very pleased with myself and my newly discovered financial discipline. I decided to show the reports to Gregory, my business accountant looking for admiration and praise. Gregory read the reports twice and then quietly looked at me and said, "I am so sorry; this is a scam. Your money did not go into a fund but into her pocket."

I fell into a chair and whispered, "How do you know that?" He then proceeded to show me the evidence in the reports. "So, my friends, I am taking a second mortgage on my place, after all."

Claire Denning, a CEO and founder of a start-up business asked, "What was her name?"

"Jackie Daniels"

Once again, the group fell silent as Lara cleared the table for dinner: a lobster bisque soup, almond crusted sea bass, asparagus spears and roasted cauliflower stems. A large pitcher of filtered water was placed on the table.

Marcie went over to Rita and put her arm around her, saying, "You are still okay with as much earning power as ever. Some lessons are very pricey."

During dinner, Claire sat next to Rita and mentioned that recently, she had a similar but weird experience in July. My yoga instructor had to leave for a week due to a serious illness in her family; her mother's stroke brought her to a nursing home in Boston. Classes were to continue with a substitute and experienced teacher. Was I ever surprised! She was even better than our regular instructor. There was a fluid motion in her postures along with a soothing and calming voice."

"Oh, I remember her," said Marcie, "when I came for a Saturday class. Yes, what a difference!"

Claire stated, "Since I live here I was able to catch all the classes that she taught. Yes, she was a melody in motion. When our regular teacher returned, I asked her for a coffee and a chat. It seems that she was planning to relocate from Colorado and currently visiting her cousins, the Clarkson's. Since I had a start-up business, I offered to help her. Y'know, press, advertising, finding the right space and meeting the right people. She was thrilled and we began to meet on a regular basis. Every town had a yoga studio, except Mid-Hampton and that was our goal."

"What did she look like?" queried Rita.

"There was an incredible presence about her; her aura was captivating. Whenever we went for coffee, people looked, both men and women. She was quite tall with long flowing blonde hair and looked marvelous in her fitness outfits, outlining every curve. Not a drop of jewelry, just an occasional scarf, a matching one at that, wrapped around her shoulders. One night we met at my house to discuss financial details."

"I am so filled with appreciation and gratitude for your interest in me. Thank you so very much."

"She actually whispered this and took my hand. I didn't realize this at first, but she was caressing my hand in hers. As soon as I was aware, I slipped my hand away, feeling an odd sensation about the whole incident. Of course, I had known that she didn't have the start-up funds so I offered seed money with a payback plan. I had a feeling that she would be very successful and I had no doubts about my offering."

Marcie was the first to question Claire further. "I am almost afraid to ask but is there a happy ending?"

"I wish I could report one. After everything was settled; rent paid advertising completed and an account set up at the bank, would you believe, I never saw her again. I went to the Clarksons with the whole story and they were as puzzled as I was. She told them she was leaving for Canada to hook up with a former lover. They just had to be together again."

Once the table was cleared and coffee was ready, Lara spoke for the first time.

"Yes, I know the Clarksons well. We have been neighbors for years and our boys were friends. We had a tennis game planned in August but due to my severely sprained ankle from my last game, I had to bow out. They brought a houseguest to take my place. What a tennis player she was, never missing a chance to score. My husband Paul was impressed with her serve and her body, I am sure. He usually doesn't like my college friends so I really didn't mind. Sailing and crewing were also her talents as I stayed home. Swimming, running and surfing were second nature to her. Was there anything that she couldn't do well, I was wondering? All of a sudden, she became our houseguest and not the Clarksons. She would bring special foods and flowers when she came. Paul was delighted with her. More than delighted; he had fallen in love with her. You see, she didn't steal money from me, she stole my husband. Twenty-seven years together with two grown sons and a wonderful life. Where was

I? What did I not see? How could I not see or feel the change in him? He is gone now, saying they have to be together. The end of this summer brings the end of my marriage."

The women sat in silence, once again hearing the same story over again. What was her name?" asked Claire.

"Candy Miller. Her name is every name and no one. She is an empty vessel and fills herself with other people's energy. Right now, my husband is filling her vessel."

"He might come back," said Marcie.

"Of course," responded Lara. "When she is finished with him."

Rita began to cry softly and said, "Oh dear Lara, I am so sorry this has happened to you. She must be so evil."

After this experience, I spoke to a colleague in the psychology department at my college. Not so much evil, but rather so sick. There is a personality disorder called multiple personality, sort of a sociopath disorder. Yes, she is all these personalities but none of them at all. She neither cares nor thinks about the damage in her wake. However, there will be a day when she will not be able to change her cover so easily. After all, we age, and in that way, she is very much like us. Except we have friends and relationships and she will have nothing. But then again, she never had anything, so there will be no loss."

The four friends finished their coffee and sat around the table quietly as the sun faded with the reminder of the summer fading as well.

Rita cheered up and said, "Hey, let's meet in the NYC next month. I found this charming bistro in the Village that you will all love. Let's celebrate each other!

Claire takes out her phone and checks the month of October. Halloween is on a Saturday and the Village parade is fun. Three other phones punch in the date... to be continued.

Jenna's Journals

Jenna was an only child of two musicians. Mom was a pianist, and Dad played the guitar. They were both alcoholics. When Jenna was an infant, her mom stayed home and only worked on weekends. Dad traveled a lot. When Jenna started school, nanny Doris came to live with them. While she had an attentive heart, she wasn't mommy.

"When is mommy coming home?" Jenna cried a lot at night. Lonely was this empty space where Jenna lived. When her parents returned, it was 'party time.' Doris took a break and Jenna joined the party. On too many occasions, someone at the party put something in her glass. She never got sick nor did she particularly like the taste of what was in the glass. What she did love was the good feelings at the party. She was adored by her parents' friends. "You are such a cutie pie. Come here and sit on my lap." She loved the hugs, kisses and the feel good caresses on her back and tummy. Jenna was 10 years old.

By the time she was in high school, Jenna had her own party group. They called themselves "The W Group," just weed and wine. At that time, Dad had found a new partner for his group, and Mom stayed home and drank, and sometimes with Jenna. One day, Jenna screamed at her, "What's the use of you being home? You're not with me. You love that bottle more than me."

After graduation, Jenna and her party friends went hip hopping across the country to California. Added to her party time, were pills and a guitarist boyfriend. Wine and weed were soon replaced by pain killers and vodka, secondary to shooting up heroin. At the very outset, she knew this was the ultimate high. She went into a different orbit, ecstasy. When Jenna returned home, she knew was in trouble with her uncontrollable heroin abuse. She didn't seek heroin addiction, but she needed a greater high. Party time was long gone, and now she was using to avoid the dreadful sickness of withdrawal. She agreed with her parents that she needed rehabilitation. On family visiting day, her only guest was her boyfriend. Dad was on tour and Mom was too sick. After completing a 28-day in patient program, she started outpatient counseling, went to meetings, found a sponsor for the difficult days, and made a commitment to live a sober life. Things were good; Jenna agreed to marry her boyfriend, and they became proud parents of a baby boy.

This was the very first time that Jenna was sober in twelve years. "I got this!" she said and left the recovery program. Larry found a spot with a trio in town and found time to be there for his wife and son. Everything was going well, except Jenna kept having reoccurring nightmares that Larry would leave her. They both agreed that she was to seek therapy. "These nightmares are from yesterday," he said, "I am not going anywhere." There were many nights when she would go to the club to hear his group. In the beginning, she just ordered a coke. When the female singer was hired, she ordered her first wine.

Larry joined Jenna in many sessions to assure her and her counselor that he was committed to his family. Once again, Jenna found nanny Doris to babysit while she went to the club. During one of her counseling sessions, she cried bitterly. "I have no talent. What can I do? Who am I?" It was a long and difficult struggle, but Jenna finally expressed an interest in writing. She enrolled in an adult writing group at the local library. Her first story of abandonment was well received by the group. Her second story of the highs and lows of substances abuse received much praise. She never wrote a third story.

Larry came home with an announcement that his group was offered a gig in Chicago. "I'll call you every night and send for you as soon as I find an apartment for us." "I know you won't," she cried, "I heard that promise before. The demons in my mind are right. You are leaving me."

There was nothing he could do to reassure her that he was committed to her and their baby.

"You are my only true love," he repeated over and over again.

Jenna left the apartment and drove to a liquor store to buy a bottle of vodka. She never returned home. The car was totaled, and Larry found her in the emergency ward at the hospital. Jenna agreed to enter a long-term care program; nanny Doris was to care for the baby and Larry went to Chicago.

Eighteen months later...

Doris has cared for the baby who is now two years old. Larry and his group have made a hit recording, and he returns every two weeks to visit Jenna on family day, and then the baby. Larry also brings the baby to visit Jenna.

Jenna has written volumes about her emotional cycles in her journals at the recovery center and the resolution of her issues in abandonment. Her counselor reports that she has made peace with her past and is now ready to establish a purpose and a goal in her life. Many of the staff have remarked on her talent to express herself.

"Do I have the right to say I am a writer if I have never been published?" she asks. Jenna has come to the conclusion that a writer is someone who writes. "Therefore, I am a writer."

When she leaves the rehabilitation center, Larry is waiting with their son. This is more than a reunion; this is a lifesaving turn of events.

While in the car, Jenna holds her baby, giving him lots of hugs and kisses. He squirms at the newness of this experience. "I know, honey. Do you wonder if I'll be there in the morning?"

She turns to Larry and says, "I need to find a direction for self-approval and not seek approval from others. I am happy you are still with me, but I must find my own source of happiness. Thank you for your support."

"Jenna, I never stopped loving you from the moment we met, and I never will."

What My Mother Forgot to Tell Me

I would like to introduce myself. My name is Zoe. I'm the eldest of two sisters, and I'm thinking of ending my life. After all, it is my life. So it's my choice. Nothing is really wrong. On the other hand, nothing is really right. My teaching job is secure in an insecure world. But my emotions well up inside me, like a dark cloud longing to be a sun. I'm a grown woman, but what's missing from my early childhood still pervades my every day. With this black, endless void inside me, consuming me from the inside out, I feel like giving up. Is this life worth living? I'm not sure. Perhaps I would feel better if I tell you my story.

My father had no formal education; his intuitive intelligence kept him afloat, for a while. My mother was a teacher of math and English. That's the right side of the brain for computing and left side for creating pictures and words. She was well ahead of her time. They were the odd couple who married and spent thirty-five years dancing around and arguing about their differences. It was difficult for married women to get a teaching job in New England; they were supposed to work at home, until World War II changed the rules. At home, she learned to cook, not gourmet; to clean, not spotlessly; to sew, not designer styles; to tend to my father's needs, wife like. I don't know if she was happy with him; no one talked to me about anything. I don't know if she was happy with her life at all.

It was clear that if she were to be my stay-at-home mother, I was to be managed and controlled as her child. All my meals were nutritious, containing the daily essential vitamins. My dresses were clean and pretty, just like a little girl should be. My schooling—both religious and secular—were rigid and observed carefully for excellent performance. My friends were from my neighborhood: clean and pretty, just like me. All of this made me feel like a puppet on a string. Why can't I eat what I want, dress how I'd like, learn what and how I want to learn? Why can't I choose whatever kind of friends I want? Why does my mother have to be in charge of every aspect of my life? Why can't I be me? Am I not good enough? I didn't want to be who she wanted me to be, I wanted to be my own person. Unfortunately, that was not the case.

Our routine life was uneventful, until my youngest sister got sick and started to fall, unable to stand. Brianna was six years old and I was ten. I was not allowed at the hospital where she was receiving treatment. "Too young" was the judgment. And I was left with my father's sisters until they returned from their visit. I was often left with Aunt Lacey because she had a son my age. Didn't anyone know that 10-year-old boys do not play with 10-year-old girls? He played ball with his friends and I read my books. When I slept over his house, we played card games and Monopoly, probably my aunt insisted. It wasn't fair. I was lonely. I needed girls my age to play with. But nobody asked me what I wanted.

Brianna was in the hospital from age six to fourteen. I didn't see my sister for eight years. What I did see was my mother's hair turn grey and my father's grim face, never smiling. There was too much stress and sadness in my household. When she was discharged and returned home, I didn't know this handicapped stranger. Although she was fourteen, Brianna looked like a very young child. They told me that she was my sister. What was I supposed to do with this new information? Who is this sister? Do I like her? She's so thin, little and crippled. No one ever explained what had happened to her. Why did I need a little sister now? What did she know about my world, my friends, our songs and dances we liked or even what we cared about? Well, it took awhile, but I finally figured it out. Brianna got all that attention for all those years while my mother left me to go to her. Of course, that was the right thing to do. And that doesn't make me feel better about Brianna or even like her.

My mother asked me to help her learn how to be with other children.

"Just take with you when you when you're with your friends. Just let her watch," implored my mother. While I did try, we were both ill-equipped for the job and I had my own girl friends in high school. No one else had to take a younger sister along. What was my mother thinking? She needn't have worried so much. Brianna did quite well in high school and on to college. Her body had been damaged by her rare disease, but her mind and intellect soared beyond anyone's expectations. She eventually earned a doctorate degree in science.

High school became more interesting for me than the restraints of the lower grades. I found outlets for my imagination and originality. I had always been attracted to off-beat ideas. My two best friends Gail and Edwina were willing to celebrate my eighteenth birthday with a daring and adventurous idea. "Let's sneak out of school and go to lunch at the diner just one block away. I look so much older now, more sophisticated. I bet I can get a cocktail," I boasted. Lunch at school was scheduled after gym class, and if we waited a few minutes, we could use that door for our escape. Giddy with excitement, we got out and ran to the restaurant. Once seated, I looked at the waitress and with the utmost confidence, I ordered "a cherry stone cocktail, please." There are no words to describe the humiliating shock when a plate of clams were placed in front of me. Grey squiggly things in a clam shell! To this day, I don't even like clams. But that experience in the restaurant was just a preview of what followed. The gym door was locked and we couldn't get in, except through the front door. Gail was the first to say, "Well, happy birthday, Zoe." Edwina echoed, "With many happy returns." Graduation was one month away, but not fast enough for me.

When I went off to college, I left the task of helping my sister's social adjustment unfinished.

During all my developing years what I missed most was my mother. Of course, I was the healthy one not needing any special attention and Brianna was always on the edge of life. Basically, I was a 'good kid,' but no one ever told me that. My mother forgot to tell me that I was valuable to her. My mother forgot to tell me that she loved me. How was I ever supposed to know? I followed her footsteps, straight into a teaching position. I even worked with children with special needs to possibly fill an unfinished job from my past. It is not possible to make up those missing eight years. They are simply gone. But the hole remains. My childhood is gone, and so is my mother who passed away many years ago. What has to happen now is I have to become the parent of me. To learn to love myself and to value my life is the next step. The struggle is constant, posing many questions of the right direction that will serve this end.

Fast forward to today.

What I have turned into is a "people pleaser," and what I neglected to do was to place myself on the list of people to be pleased. I put a smile on because no one likes a long face. I dress fashionably. When burgundy was in, I wore it. Whether skirts were long or short, I followed the trend. People like to see color and style. To be nice is my mantra, always finding a complement for other people. What's wrong with being "nice?" Why doesn't that make me feel good about myself?

My relationship with my boyfriend, Colin—now called my significant other because we live together—is comfortable. He keeps his apartment, sublet to a friend, just in case we split. I don't want to be stuck with anyone for any reason, and I insisted he keep that option available. Not much of a commitment on my part, but he has accepted it. The paramount issue is his messiness. He doesn't care about order, cleanliness and neatness. And then, it becomes my responsibility alone to keep our living space acceptable to me. I like being with him. He's funny, kind and carefree. Most of the time, he's very loving and sex is good. Can he be all these things and still remember to put the cap on the toothpaste?

Just one month ago, a small argument about his dirty socks escalated into a huge fight about my obsessive controlling personality. He threw his things into his bags and left. I don't know why I didn't cry. It's lonely without him. Why does anyone have to apologize for who they are or who they are not? One of us has to call or this is the end.

While writing my story, I opened the Concise Oxford Dictionary, 1990 edition, to discover there were only three pages of words beginning with the letter Z while there were dozens and dozens of pages with words beginning with the letter B. Last again! Am I still looking for praise and acknowledgement that I am valuable and worthwhile? Someone has to do this for me. I guess it has to be me. In order to build up my self esteem and feel more worthwhile, I must do activities that are worthy and valuable, to be determined by myself. Where to begin? It's late. Work tomorrow. I'm going to sleep.

For the next few days, I am busy with friends and school activities, with no plan to boost my self-esteem. I woke up early one Saturday morning, sat upright in bed and said aloud, "It's my turn. Time for me." I put on my tights and a tee, and drove to the community center to sign up for a beginner's yoga class. I went up to the instructor and confessed, "I'm new to this class. I don't know what to do." The teacher smiled warmly responded, "You'll be fine. Just relax and breathe. Do as much of the postures as you feel comfortable. No pain here; just a stretch or two." I looked around the room that was bathed in morning light as the multi-colored yoga mats were placed on the floor. All sizes, shapes and ages were here. Lots of beginners today. The music was soothing and invited me to an imaginary place. The yoga teacher was offering an invitation: "You are in your imaginary garden. Notice what you can see both near and far. What aromas can you smell? What can you touch with your fingertips and what can you feel with your bare feet? How does the breeze caress your cheeks? What sounds can you hear both distant and near? In your private garden, say to yourself, I am a lovable and loving person."

During the resting period at the end of class, I felt strangely comfortable and wondered why tears were rolling down my cheeks.

I thought, "Yes, I am a very special Zoe today." I was just with me and that was very special. Perhaps I can create a life worth living. And thanks for listening.

The Fifty-Minute Hour…Fridays @ 5

Pamela was always on time. When the doctor opened the door, she was eager to enter. Sitting on the plush, beige loveseat and resting against the paisley print pillow, she began: "I cycled twenty-five miles last Saturday; it was so exhilarating. I love the wind blowing through my hair and brushing against my arms and legs. When I tighten my stomach muscles, I can move my legs faster; it's orgasmic. The freedom I feel; it is worth getting up at the crack of dawn so the road can be mine. I cycled twenty-five miles both ways; now I am ready for a fifty-mile trip. I come home tired, but my body is singing; every part is humming. It's so good to be alive."

The doctor listened but gazed at the furniture, and then back to Pamela who was wearing a low cut snug tee shirt with tight fitting jeans and white sneakers. The room is comforting in different shades of beige, low lighting, and a soft brown carpet. A large glass table holds a water pitcher, cups, and the omnipresent tissue box to catch uncontrollable emotions. The doctor encourages emotions to flow.

Pamela picks up the pace of her dialogue to describe the invitation she received to join a bike club, and why she turned it down. Her tone changed, almost to a whisper as she leaned forward revealing the soft fullness of her breasts.

"I cannot function in a group. I need to ride solo. And yet, I would like a cycling partner but not just anyone. It would have to be someone special. I would like someone who…"

Pamela stopped talking and looked directly at the doctor whose gaze fled to the flowers in the vase. The yellow and orange tiger lilies were the only color in the room. A few were standing tall and straight but for how long would they last, the doctor wondered.

Pamela went on to describe her mother's birthday party with her two sisters whom she could barely tolerate. The doctor knew that she was trying to improve her relations with her family and create some level of harmony. Her blonde curls bounced on her shoulders when she spoke about this conflict. The doctor wondered just how soft her curls were. The fantasy of touching her curls and winding them around her fingertips became unbearable, and the doctor shifted her position in a brown, leather chair. It was agony waiting for 5:50, but it finally came.

Pamela got up and said, "See you next Friday. By the way, do you have any open appointments; I would like to come twice a week?"

Pamela had been a patient in this office for three months. She had been referred to the therapist by the school psychologist where she was teaching kindergarten.

The doctor responded firmly, "Not at this time."

Pamela accepted this response and left quietly, without her usual fuss, asking if she could call if something came up. Pamela was a 29-year-old, a single woman who was new to the process of psychotherapy. She was raised in the Bahamas by two professional parents who had little time for their youngest daughter. She was often in the care of a sitter or her two older sisters. She found many playmates on the island, both girlfriends and boyfriends. Her sensual beauty and playful nature attracted many companions. When she was eighteen, her family migrated to New York, and Pamela found a roommate who was both a mentor and a lover while she attended classes. She identified herself as bisexual, but had a preference for women.

Dr. Lauren Gruen has been a practicing analyst for seventeen years in an office and apartment in Central Park West. She had a thriving practice and was known for her insight and intelligent analysis. She never had experienced any personal interest in any client, other than an accurate diagnosis with progress toward optimal mental and emotional health, until now!

Pamela's sensual beauty and provocative nature captured her personal interest at the onset. She found Pamela to be interesting and then surprisingly, appealing. Appealing to what? While she knew Pamela to be bisexual, Lauren Gruen was not. She felt composed and controlled in all of her therapeutic sessions. If she finds Pamela attractive and compelling, what is the nature of that interest?

Lauren Gruen was more than satisfied with her life, her friendships and especially her significant other, a successful businessman. While she did have a supervising analyst to whom she could turn to for difficult cases, this was not the one.

She walked to the window to watch Pamela stroll down the street with her pocketbook swinging from her left shoulder. She had a brisk walk, and today she swayed into the park. Lauren rubbed her temple and thought that she cannot continue with her. She must end the sessions without being hurtful. I'll tell her that I have a conference out of town and then travel. I'll give her a referral that would be just right. This would be best for both of us.

Friday at five: Dr. Gruen opens the door and finds Pamela waiting as beautiful as ever. Today she is donning a floral swing skirt with a sleeveless v-neck shirt and sandals. The v cut is deep enough to sport a full cleavage. Her tawny skin was shining with a slight golden tan. The doctor was determined to say something today. She must.

Pamela flounced on the couch and began to describe her fifty-mile trip with a stay in a local hotel at the end of her road trip.

"Imagine me on such a long trip alone, to the end of the island. Imagine me, alone. This trip was one with fatigue and excitement. Once settled in the motel right on the ocean, I showered and fell on the crisp white linen sheets listening to the rhythm of the waves cresting and falling on the shore. My body moved with each wave, up and then down. It was pure heaven. I fell asleep and awoke in a dreamy state. I got up and dressed; I went to a local pub for food and fun."

Dr. Lauren Gruen listened to Pamela's oceanic orgasmic experience. She couldn't move or speak. She just watched Pamela move as she acted out her trip.

Did Pamela know? Lauren was wet.

For a few minutes, no one spoke as Pamela looked directly at her. Finally she said, "I know my time is up. I'll just go and see you next week."

Lauren quickly responded, "Wait; don't go yet. There is something I need to tell you."

Pamela leaned forward to hear, once again revealing her full breasts through the opening in her blouse.

"I need to tell you that I'll be out of the office for several months. First, I have a conference that I must attend, and then travel. It would be best if you see someone else at this time, since I am not certain about my return date,"

She gave her a card and insisted that this therapist, a colleague, would be good for her.

Pamela took the card and said that she probably would not call the other therapist, but would wait for Lauren's return.

Dr. Lauren responded, "It's your choice. I hope our work together has been somewhat helpful to you."

Pamela nodded and said, "Have a good trip. Thanks."

Pamela left and once again Lauren walked to the window to see her walk away. Tears rolled down her cheeks and she said aloud, "I made it; I am okay. It was just a feeling, a passing sensation. It was not who I am. It's okay to have many feelings, and this will pass."

Lauren doesn't have any words to describe the feelings. It all seemed to be beyond her control.

She went back to her desk and closed the file.

Acknowledgements

Thank you to Michele Gottlieb for her thoughtful editing. To Alena Joy Berenblatt for her loving patience. And to Chloë and Paige Bzdyk for their support in all of my endeavors.

About the Author

Maida Berenblatt, M.S., is a Professor in Psychology at Suffolk County Community College, Selden, New York, and a Family Counselor at Seafield Center, a treatment center for the rehabilitation of alcohol and drug addiction in Westhampton Beach, New York. Maida has co-authored two books with her daughter Alena Joy Berenblatt, *Make An Appointment With Yourself, Simple Steps To Positive Self-Esteem*, which was featured on OPRAH and *Changeweavers: A Pathway to Spiritual Renewal*.

81119121R00031